POE
Illustrated

THREE STORIES BY
EDGAR ALLAN POE

ADAPTED BY:
JEROME TILLER
ILLUSTRATED BY:
MARC JOHNSON-PENCOOK

T0243155

The *Adapted Classics* Collection

Contemporary-classic illustrations in *Adapted Classics* books add expression to visually-rich stories by world-famous authors. Lightly modified and illustrated to suit and attract modern young readers, stories in the *Adapted Classics* collection are respectful renditions of timeless stories from the world of classic literature.

View the entire collection at: www.adaptedclassics.com

PREFACE

You are about to read adapted versions of three stories by Edgar Allan Poe, one of the world's all-time greatest authors. Some changes (paragraph breaks, rearrangements, minor additions and omissions, etc.) were made to accommodate the illustration of characters and critical scenes in the story. Some changes (word choice, word order, minor additions, etc.) were made to expand its accessibility and appeal, keeping modern youth in mind. No change was made with the notion it would improve the text or the story.

Among other places, the original version of each story can be found at: http://www. gutenberg.org/

CONTENTS

THOU ART THE MAN

Mr. Barnabas Shuttleworthy—one of the wealthiest and most respectable citizens in Rattleborough— had set out from town very early one Saturday morning on horseback with the avowed intention of proceeding to the city of Ruxbridge, about fifteen miles distant, and of returning home on the night of the same day.

Two hours after Mr. Shuttleworthy's departure, however, his horse returned without him, and also without the saddlebags that had been strapped on its back. The animal was wounded, too, and covered with mud. These circumstances naturally gave rise to much alarm among the friends of the missing man. When he had not yet made his appearance on Sunday morning, the citizens of the town arose en masse to go and look for his body.

The foremost and most energetic in beginning this search was the bosom friend of Mr. Shuttleworthy—a Mr. Charles Goodfellow, or, as he was universally called, "Charley Goodfellow," or "Old Charley Goodfellow".

Now, I have never been able to figure out why, but the fact is unquestionable that never yet was there any person named Charles who was not an open, manly, honest, good-natured, and frank-hearted fellow, with a rich, clear voice that did you good to hear it, and an eye that looked you always straight in the face inasmuch as to say: "I have a clear conscience myself, am afraid of no man, and am altogether above doing a mean action."

"Old Charley Goodfellow," had been in Rattleborough not longer than six months, and although nobody knew anything about him before he came to settle in the neighborhood, he experienced no difficulty in making the acquaintance of all the respectable people in the town. Every man among them would have taken his bare word for a thousand at any moment. As for the women, there is no telling what they would not have done to oblige him. And all this came about because he had been christened Charles, and because he possessed, in consequence, that sincere face which is proverbially the very "best letter of recommendation".

THOU ART THE MAN

I have already said that Mr. Shuttleworthy was most respectable and, undoubtedly, the wealthiest man in Rattleborough, while "Old Charley Goodfellow" got along with him as intimately as if he had been his own brother. The two old gentlemen were next-door neighbors, and, although Mr. Shuttleworthy seldom, if ever, visited "Old Charley", and never was known to take a meal in his house, this did not prevent the two friends from being exceedingly close. "Old Charley" never let a day pass without stepping in three or four times to see how his neighbor was. Very often he would stay to breakfast or tea, and almost always to dinner, and at these sittings the amount of wine the two old cronies put down would really be hard to ascertain.

"Old Charley's" favorite beverage was Chateau-Margaux, and it appeared to do Mr. Shuttleworthy's heart good to see the old fellow swallow it, as he did, quart after quart. One day, with the wine in them and their wits naturally somewhat out, Mr. Shuttleworthy slapped his crony upon the back.

"I tell you what it is, 'Old Charley'", he said. "You are, by all odds, the heartiest old fellow I ever came across in all my born days. And since you love to guzzle the wine like you do, I'll be darned if I don't have to make you a present of a big box of the Chateau-Margaux."

"By gosh", continued Mr. Shuttleworthy, "I'm gonna send an order to town this very afternoon for a double box of the best that can be got, and I'll make you a present of it, I will! Ya needn't say a word now. I will, I tell ya. So look out for it. It will come to pass one of these fine days, precisely when you are looking for it the least!"

This little bit of generosity on the part of Mr. Shuttleworthy shows how very intimate an understanding existed between the two friends.

On the Sunday morning in question, when it came to be fairly understood that Mr. Shuttleworthy had met with foul play, I never saw anyone so profoundly affected as "Old Charley Goodfellow".

When he first heard that the horse had come home without his master, and without his master's saddlebags, and all bloody from a pistol shot that had gone clean through and through the poor animal's chest without quite killing it, Charley turned as pale as if the missing man had been his own dear brother or father, and shivered and shook all over as if he had had a fit of chills and fever.

At first he was much too overpowered with grief to be able to do any thing at all, or to agree upon any plan of action. For a long time he endeavored to dissuade Mr. Shuttleworthy's other friends from making a stir about the matter. He thought it best to wait awhile, say for a week or two, or a month, or two months, to see if something wouldn't turn up, or if Mr. Shuttleworthy wouldn't come in the natural way and explain his reasons for sending his horse home before him.

People who are laboring under very poignant sorrow have often been observed to stall or procrastinate like this. Their powers of mind seem to be rendered slow and dull, so that they have a horror of anything like action. People in this state like nothing in the world so much as to lie quietly in bed and "nurse their grief", as some old folks express it—that is to say, repeatedly turn the trouble over in their mind.

The people of Rattleborough had indeed so high an opinion of the wisdom and discretion of "Old Charley", that the greater part of them felt disposed to agree with him, and not make a stir in the business "until something should turn up", as the honest old gentleman worded it.

It is likely this would have been the general determination except for the very suspicious interference of Mr. Shuttleworthy's nephew, Pennifeather. He was a young man of very wasteful habits and otherwise a rather bad character. This nephew would listen to nothing like reason in the matter of "lying quiet", but insisted upon making immediate search for the "corpse of the murdered man". This was the expression he employed, and Mr. Goodfellow acutely remarked at the time that it was "a singular expression, to say no more".

This remark of "Old Charley's" also had great effect upon the crowd, and one of the party was heard to ask, very impressively, "how it happened that young Mr. Pennifeather was so intimately aware of all the circumstances connected with his wealthy uncle's disappearance as to feel authorized to assert, distinctly and decisively, that his uncle was 'a murdered man'". Hereupon some bickering occurred among various members of the crowd, and especially between "Old Charley" and Mr. Pennifeather.

This confrontation between"Old Charley" and Mr. Pennifeather was, indeed, by no means a novelty, for no good will had existed between them for the last three or four months. Matters had even gone so far that Mr. Pennifeather had actually knocked down his uncle's friend for some alleged excess of liberty that "Old Charley" had taken in his uncle's house where the nephew was residing.

Upon this occasion "Old Charley" is said to have behaved with commendable moderation and Christian charity. He arose from the blow, adjusted his clothes, and made no attempt to retaliate at all—merely muttering a few words about "taking summary vengeance at the first convenient opportunity",—a natural and very justifiable outburst of anger which meant nothing, however, and beyond doubt, was no sooner vented than forgotten.

However these matters may be (which have no reference to the point now at issue), it is quite certain that the people of Rattleborough, principally through the persuasion of Mr. Pennifeather, at length decided to disperse over the adjacent country in search of the missing Mr. Shuttleworthy.

I say this is what they decided to do at first. After it had been fully resolved that a search should be made, it was considered almost a matter of course that the seekers should disperse—that is to say, distribute themselves in parties—for the more thorough examination of the region round about. I forget, however, by what ingenious train of reasoning it was that "Old Charley" finally convinced the assembly that this was the most unsound plan that could be pursued. Convince them, however, he did—all except Mr. Pennifeather, and, in the end, it was arranged that a search should begin, carefully and very thoroughly, by the townsfolk en masse with "Old Charley" himself leading the way.

As for the matter of that, there could have been no better pioneer than "Old Charley", whom everybody knew to have the eye of a lynx, but although he led them into all manner of out-of-the-way holes and corners, by routes that nobody had ever suspected of existing in the neighborhood, and although the search was incessantly kept up day and night for nearly a week, still no trace of Mr. Shuttleworthy could be discovered.

When I say no trace, however, I must not be understood to speak literally, for to some extent there certainly was a trace. The poor gentleman had been tracked by his horse's shoes

(which were peculiar) to a spot about three miles to the east of the town on the main road leading to the city. Here the track made off into a by-path through a piece of woodland—the path coming out again into the main road and cutting off about half a mile of the regular distance.

Following the shoe-marks down this lane, the party came at length to a pool of stagnant water, half hidden by the brambles. To the right of the lane and opposite this pool all trace of the track was lost sight of. It appeared, however, that a struggle of some nature had here taken place, and it seemed as if some large and heavy body, much larger and heavier than a man, had been drawn from the by-path to the pool.

This pool was carefully dragged twice, but nothing was found, and the party was about to go away in despair when Providence suggested to Mr. Goodfellow the appropriateness of draining the water off altogether. This project was received with cheers and with many high compliments to "Old Charley" for his wisdom and consideration.

As many of the townspeople had brought spades with them, supposing that they might possibly be called upon to dig up a corpse, the drain was easily and speedily accomplished, and no sooner was the bottom visible, than right in the middle of the mud that remained was discovered a black silk velvet waistcoat, which nearly every one present immediately recognized as the property of Mr. Pennifeather.

This waistcoat was much torn and stained with blood, and there were several persons among the party who had a distinct remembrance of its having been worn by its owner on the very morning of Mr. Shuttleworthy's departure for the city. There were others, again, ready to testify upon oath, if required, that Mr. P. did not wear the garment in question at any period during the remainder of that memorable day, nor could any one be found to say that he had seen Mr. P. wear the garment at any time after Mr. Shuttleworthy's disappearance.

Matters now wore a very serious aspect for Mr. Pennifeather. He grew exceedingly pale, and when asked what he had to say for himself, he was utterly incapable of saying a word. Mr. P's riotous mode of living had left him but a few friends, and they to a man, upon observing his reaction to this discovery of the vest, deserted him at once and, even more than his ancient and avowed enemies, clamored for his instantaneous arrest.

But, on the other hand, in contrast with the clamoring crowd, the high-mindedness of Mr. Goodfellow shone forth with all the more brilliant luster. He made a warm and intensely eloquent defense of Mr. Pennifeather, in which he alluded more than once to his own sincere forgiveness of that wild young gentleman, "the heir of the worthy Mr. Shuttleworthy", for the insult which Mr. Pennifeather had, no doubt in the heat of passion, thought proper to put upon him.

"I forgave him for it", Mr. Goodfellow said, "from the very bottom of my heart. And rather than push the present suspicious circumstances to extremes, circumstances which I am sorry to say really have arisen against Mr. Pennifeather, I will instead do everything in my power, will employ all the little eloquence in my possession to–to–to soften down, as much as I can conscientiously do, the worst features of this really exceedingly perplexing piece of business."

Mr. Goodfellow went on for some half hour longer in this strain, very much to the credit both of his head and his heart. But such warm-hearted people as he, in the hot-headedness of their zeal to serve a friend, are seldom appropriate in their observations—they run into all sorts of blunders, awkward mishaps and ludicrous misuse of words. Thus, often with the kindest intentions in the world, they do infinitely more to prejudice a friend's cause than to advance it.

In the present instance, so it did turn out with all the eloquence of "Old Charley". For, although he labored earnestly on behalf of the suspected, somehow or other every syllable he uttered had the effect to deepen the suspicion already attached to the individual whose cause he pleaded and to arouse against him the fury of the mob.

One of the most unaccountable errors committed by the orator was his allusion to the suspected as "the heir of the worthy old gentleman Mr. Shuttleworthy". The people had never thought of this before. They had only remembered certain threats of disinheritance uttered a year or two previously by the uncle (who had no living relative except the nephew), and they had, therefore, always looked upon this disinheritance as a matter that was settled.

But the remark by "Old Charley" brought them at once to a consideration of this point, and it helped them to see the possibility that Mr. Shuttleworthy's threats had in fact been nothing more than threats. And straightway there arose the natural question of "who stands to gain from this?"—a question that tended even more than the bloody vest to fasten the terrible crime upon the young man.

Now in the present instance, the question "who stands to gain" very pointedly implicated Mr. Pennifeather. His uncle had threatened him, after making a will in his favor, with disinheritance. But the threat had not been actually kept; the original will, it appeared, had not been altered. Had it been altered, the only supposable motive for murder on the part of the suspected would have been the ordinary one of revenge, and even this would have been counteracted by the hope of

restoration into the good graces of the uncle. But the will being unaltered, while the threat to alter it remained suspended over the nephew's head, suggested at once the very strongest possible motive for the atrocity, and so concluded, very wisely, the worthy citizens of Rattleborough.

Mr. Pennifeather was, accordingly, arrested on the spot, and the crowd, after some further search, proceeded homeward having him in custody. On the route, however, another circumstance occurred tending to confirm the suspicion they entertained.

Mr. Goodfellow, whose zeal led him to be always a little in advance of the party, was seen suddenly to run forward a few paces, stoop, and then to pick up some small object from the grass. After quickly examining it, he was observed to make an attempt, or sort of half-attempt, at concealing in his coat pocket what he had found, but this action was noticed, as I say, and consequently prevented, when the object picked up was found to be a Spanish knife which a dozen persons at once recognized as belonging to Mr. Pennifeather. Moreover, his initials were engraved upon the handle. The blade of this knife was open and bloody.

Now no doubt remained of the guilt of the nephew, and immediately upon reaching Rattleborough, he was taken

before a judge for examination. Here matters again took a most unfavorable turn. The prisoner, being questioned as to his whereabouts on the morning of Mr. Shuttleworthy's disappearance, had the absolute audacity to acknowledge that on that very morning he had been out with his rifle deer-stalking in the immediate neighborhood of the pool where the blood-stained waistcoat had been discovered through the wisdom of Mr. Goodfellow.

Mr. Goodfellow now came forward and, with tears in his eyes, asked permission to be examined by the judge. He said the stern sense of the duty that he owed his Maker, not less than his fellow-men, would no longer permit him to remain silent. He said that, before now, his sincerest affection for the young man (notwithstanding the ill-treatment he had received from him) had induced him to imagine every possible thing that might account for all the suspicious circumstances that appeared to point to Mr. Pennifeather. But, he said, these circumstances were now altogether too convincing—too damning. He would hesitate no longer—he would tell all he knew, although his heart should absolutely burst asunder in the effort.

Mr. Goodfellow then went on to swear that on the afternoon of the day before Mr. Shuttleworthy departed for the city, he had heard that worthy old gentleman mention to his nephew that he was going to town the next day to make a deposit of an unusually large sum of money in the "Farmers and Mechanics' Bank", and that during the same conversation Mr. Shuttleworthy had also distinctly informed his nephew that he had irrevocably decided to cancel the original will and cut him off without a shilling. Mr. Goodfellow now solemnly called upon the accused to state whether this was or was not the truth in every substantial particular. Much to the astonishment of every one present, Mr. Pennifeather frankly admitted that it was.

The judge now considered it his duty to send a couple of constables to search the chamber of the accused in the house of his uncle, and they almost immediately returned with the well-known steel-bound, russet leather pocket-book that the old gentleman had been in the habit of carrying for years. Its valuable contents, however, had been removed.

The judge tried to make the prisoner state what use he had made of the contents or in which place they had been concealed, but Mr. Pennifeather obstinately denied all knowledge of the matter. The constables also produced a shirt and handkerchief that they had found between the bed and mattress of the victim. Both articles were marked with B.S., the initials of his name, and both hideously besmeared with his blood.

At this juncture, it was announced that the horse of the murdered man had just died in the stable from the effects of the wound it had received. Upon hearing this, Mr. Goodfellow proposed that a post mortem examination of the beast should be immediately made, with the view, if possible, of discovering the bullet.

This was accordingly done and, as if to demonstrate beyond a question the guilt of the accused, Mr. Goodfellow, after considerable searching in the cavity of the horse's chest, was able to detect and pull forth a bullet of very extraordinary size. Upon testing, this bullet was found to be exactly adapted to the bore of Mr. Pennifeather's rifle, while it was far too large to fit the rifle of any other person in the town or its vicinity.

To render the matter even surer yet, however, this bullet was discovered to have a flaw or seam at right angles to the usual seam. Upon examination, this seam corresponded precisely with an accidental ridge in a pair of bullet molds that the accused admitted owning and regularly using to manufacture bullets for his unusual rifle.

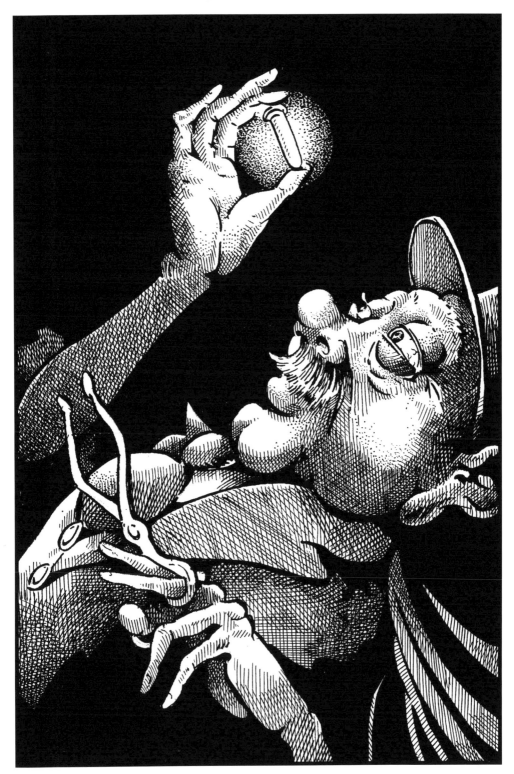

Upon discovery of this evidence, the examining judge refused to listen to any further testimony. He immediately committed the prisoner for trial and firmly declined to take any bail in the case, although Mr. Goodfellow very warmly complained against this severe restriction and solemnly offered to post bond in whatever amount might be required.

This generosity on the part of "Old Charley" was only in keeping with his friendly and gracious conduct during the entire period of his temporary stay in Rattleborough. In this particular display of his virtuous conduct, the worthy Mr. Goodfellow was so entirely carried away by the warmth of his sympathy that, when he offered to put up bail for his young friend, he seemed to have quite forgotten that he did not possess a single dollar's worth of property upon the face of the earth.

The result of the judge's committal of Mr. Pennifeather may be easily foreseen. Amid the loud cursings of all Rattleborough, he was brought to trial at the next criminal sessions. The chain of circumstantial evidence (strengthened as it was by some additional damning facts from Mr. Goodfellow, whose sensitive conscientiousness forbade him to withhold evidence from the court) was considered so unbroken and so thoroughly conclusive that the jury returned an immediate verdict of "Guilty of murder in the first degree."

Soon afterward the unhappy wretch received the
sentence of death, and he was remanded to the
county jail to await the unchangeable vengeance of
the law.

In the meantime, the noble behavior of "Old Charley"
Goodfellow had doubly endeared him to the honest
citizens of Rattleborough. He became ten times a
greater favorite than ever, and, as a natural result of
the hospitality with which he was treated, he relaxed
the extremely stingy habits which his poverty had,
until now, impelled him to observe. Very frequently
he had little reunions at his own house when wit
and gaiety reigned supreme—dampened a little,
of course, by the occasional remembrance of the
unfortunate and melancholy fate which hovered over
the nephew of the late lamented bosom friend of the
generous host.

One fine day, this noble old gentleman was agreeably surprised at the receipt of the following letter:

To: Charles Goodfellow, Esq., Rattleborough
From: H.F.B. & Co. Chateau-Margaux

A — No. 1.— 6 doz. bottles (1/2 Gross)

Charles Goodfellow, Esquire

Dear Sir:

In conformity with an order transmitted to our firm about two months since by our esteemed correspondent, Mr. Barnabus Shuttleworthy, we have the honor this morning of forwarding to your address a double box of Chateau-Margaux of the antelope brand, violet seal. Box numbered and marked as per margin.

We remain, sir,

Your most obedient servants,

HOGGS, FROGS, BOGS, & CO

P.S. The box will reach you by wagon on the day after your receipt of this letter. Our respects to Mr. Shuttleworthy.
"H., F., B., & CO."

Since the death of Mr. Shuttleworthy, Mr. Goodfellow had given up all expectation of ever receiving the promised Chateau-Margaux. Therefore, he now looked upon it as a sort of exceptional distribution of Providence on his behalf. He was highly delighted, of course, and in the exuberance of his joy, he invited a large party of friends to a small supper on the very next day for the purpose of cracking open the good old Mr. Shuttleworthy's present.

Not that he said anything about "the good old Mr. Shuttleworthy" when he issued the invitations. The fact is, he thought much about it and concluded to say nothing at all. He did not mention to any one—if I remember right—that he had received a present of Chateau-Margaux. He merely asked his friends to come and help him drink some wine of a remarkable fine quality and rich flavor that he had ordered up from the city a couple of months ago and that he would receive the day of the supper.

I have often puzzled myself over why "Old Charley" had decided to say nothing about having received the wine from his old friend, but I could never precisely understand his reason for the silence, although he had some excellent and very high-minded reason, no doubt.

A very large and highly respectable company showed up at Mr. Goodfellow's house when the next day arrived. Indeed, half the town of Rattlesborough was there—I myself among the number—but, much to the irritation of the host, the Chateau-Margaux arrived late, and not until the guests had finished the sumptuous supper "Old Charley" had prepared for them. It came at length, however, and a monstrously big box of it there was, too. Since everyone was in excessively good humor, it was decided, unanimously, that the box should be lifted upon the table and its contents removed without delay.

No sooner said than done. I lent a helping hand and, in a flash, we had the box upon the table and amongst all the bottles and glasses, not a few of which were demolished in the scuffle. "Old Charley," who was pretty much intoxicated and excessively red in the face, took a seat. With an air of mock dignity he sat at the head of the table and thumped furiously upon it with a decanter, calling upon the company to keep order "during the ceremony of disinterring the treasure."

After some clamor, quiet was at length fully restored and, as often happens in similar cases, a profound and remarkable silence ensued. Being then requested to force open the lid, I complied "with an infinite deal of pleasure". I inserted a chisel, and giving it a few slight taps with a hammer, the top of the box flew suddenly

off. At the same instant, there sprang up into a sitting position, directly facing the host, the bruised, bloody, and nearly putrid corpse of the murdered Mr. Shuttleworthy himself. The corpse gazed for a few seconds, fixedly and sorrowfully, and with its decaying and lackluster eyes full into the face of Mr. Goodfellow, it uttered slowly, but clearly and impressively, the words "Thou art the man!" Then, falling over the side of the chest as if thoroughly satisfied, it stretched out its limbs quiveringly upon the table.

The scene that came afterward is altogether beyond description. The rush for the doors and windows was terrific, and many of the most robust men in the room fainted outright through sheer horror. But after the first wild, shrieking burst of fright, all eyes were directed to Mr. Goodfellow.

If I live a thousand years, I can never forget the more than mortal agony which was depicted in that ghastly face of his so lately flushed red with triumph and wine. For several minutes he sat rigidly as a statue of marble, his eyes seeming, in the intense vacancy of their gaze, to be turned inward and absorbed in the contemplation of his own miserable, murderous soul. At length the expression in his eyes appeared to flash out into the external world, when, with a quick leap he sprang from his chair, and falling heavily with his head and shoulders upon the table, and in contact with the corpse, poured out rapidly and vehemently a detailed confession of the hideous crime for which Mr. Pennifeather had been imprisoned and doomed to die.

In substance what he recounted was this: He followed his victim to the vicinity of the pool; there shot his horse with a pistol, dispatched its rider with the butt end, possessed himself of the pocket-book, and, supposing the horse dead, dragged it with great labor to the brambles by the pond. Upon his own beast he slung the corpse of Mr. Shuttleworthy and thus bore it to a secure place of concealment a long distance off through the woods. The waistcoat, the knife, the pocket-book, and bullet had been placed by himself where found with the view of avenging himself upon Mr. Pennifeather. He had also plotted the discovery of the stained handkerchief and shirt.

Towards the end of this blood-churning recital, the words of the guilty wretch faltered and grew hollow. When the record was finally exhausted, he arose, staggered backward from the table, and fell dead.

Although efficient, the means by which I extorted this happily-timed confession were simple indeed. Mr. Goodfellow's excess frankness had disgusted me and excited my suspicions from the first. I was also present when Mr. Pennifeather struck him and knocked him down, and the fiendish expression which arose then upon the face of "Old Charley", although momentary, assured me that his threat of vengeance would, if possible, be rigidly fulfilled. I was thus prepared to view the maneuvering of "Old Charley" in a very different light from that in which the good citizens of Rattleborough regarded it.

I saw at once that all the incriminating discoveries arose, either directly or indirectly, from himself. But the fact which clearly opened my eyes to the true state of the case was the affair of the bullet found by Mr. G. in the carcass of the horse. I had not forgotten, although the citizens had, that there was a hole where the ball had entered the horse and another where it went out. If it were found in the animal then, after having made its exit, I saw clearly that it must have been deposited by the person who found it.

The bloody shirt and handkerchief confirmed the idea suggested by the bullet, for the blood on examination proved to be claret red wine and no more. When I came to think of these things, and also of the late increase of liberality and expenditure on the part of Mr. Goodfellow, I entertained a suspicion which was none the less strong because I kept it altogether to myself.

In the meantime, I instituted a rigorous private search for the corpse of Mr. Shuttleworthy and, for good reasons, searched in quarters as divergent as possible from those to which Mr. Goodfellow conducted his party. The result was that, after some days, I came across an old dry well, the mouth of which was nearly hidden by brambles; here, at the bottom, I discovered what I sought.

Now it so happened that I had overheard the conversation between the two cronies, when Mr. Shuttleworthy promised Mr. Goodfellow a box of Chateaux-Margaux.

Upon this hint I acted. I procured a length of supple whalebone and thrust it down the throat of the corpse. I then deposited the corpse in an old wine box—taking care to double up the body so as to also double up the whalebone, which loaded tension into it. Having done this, I had to press forcibly upon the lid to keep it down while I secured the lid with nails. I anticipated, of course, that as soon as the nails were removed, the top would fly off and the body up.

Having thus arranged the box, I marked, numbered, and addressed it as already told. And then, writing a letter in the name of the wine merchants with whom Mr. Shuttleworthy dealt, I gave instructions to my servant to wheel the box to Mr. Goodfellow's door in a barrow at a given signal from myself. For the words which I intended the corpse to speak, I confidently depended upon my polished abilities as an amateur ventriloquist. For the effect of those words, I counted upon the conscience of the murderous wretch.

I believe there is nothing more to be explained. Mr. Pennifeather was released upon the spot, inherited the fortune of his uncle, profited by the lessons of experience, turned over a new leaf, and led happily ever afterward a new life.

the end

THOU ART THE MAN

Despite being praised by one critic as a 'trail blazing tour de force', most Poe admirers discount *Thou Art the Man* as one of his lesser efforts. It is said that Poe wrote this story in 1845 as an experiment in detective writing, the category of fiction that he himself invented. Though it may be flawed in many reader's minds, it deserves much credit for its merits and innovations.

It is, after all, the first story in which a character uses the science of ballistics to explain a crime, and it's the first mystery in which the culprit turned out to be "the least likely suspect". It is also the first time a fictional character used a trick—ventriloquism—to fool a suspect into confessing to a crime. Tricks to force a confession have been used many times since by mystery writers when they create stories that do not contain sufficient real evidence to link criminals to their crimes.

Moreover, Poe used two other unusual features to advance this detective story. He has two different characters—Charley Goodfellow and the narrator—produce two different lines of reasoning, false and true, to explain the death of the victim. And the narrator—who is an amateur detective—must hold the reader in suspense describing a mystery that he has already solved while simultaneously revealing the clues readers would need to solve the mystery on their own.

Finally, and most important, "Thou Art the Man" is the first comic detective story. Though too rarely credited for his sense of humor, Poe utilized his sharp, devilish wit in most of his stories. In "Thou Art the Man", he uses satire to humorously shred the gullible townsfolk who so faithfully follow the highly suspicious advice and false leads of good ol' Charley Goodfellow.

HOP-FROG

No one was ever so keenly alive to a joke as the king was. He seemed to live only for joking. About the refinements of wit, the king troubled himself very little— over-niceties wearied him. He had a special admiration for the big joke and would often put up with a long lead-in to the punch line for the sake of it. To tell a good story of the joking kind, and to tell it well, was a sure road to his favor, although, upon the whole, practical jokes suited his taste far better than verbal ones. Thus it happened that his seven ministers were all noted for their accomplishments as jokers, excelling both at verbal jokes and jokes of the practical kind. They all took after the king, too, in being large, corpulent, oily men.

This was a time when professional jesters had not altogether gone out of fashion at court. Several of the great continental 'powers' retained 'fools', who wore caps with bells and were expected to always be ready with sharp witticisms at a moment's notice in consideration of the crumbs that fell from the royal table.

Our king then, as a matter of course, retained a fool, or professional jester. The fool's name was Hop-Frog. But Hop-Frog was not only a fool; his value was trebled in the eyes of the king by the fact he was also a dwarf and a cripple. In those days dwarfs were as common at court as fools, and many monarchs would have found it difficult to get through their days (days are rather longer at court than elsewhere) without both a jester to laugh with and a dwarf to laugh at.

I believe the name 'Hop-Frog' was not the name given to the dwarf by his sponsors at baptism, but it was conferred upon him, by general consent of the several ministers, on account of his inability to walk as other men do. In fact, Hop-Frog could only get along by a sort of halting gait—something between a leap and a wriggle—a movement that afforded unlimited amusement to the king.

But although Hop-Frog, through the distortion of his legs, could move only with great pain and difficulty along a road or floor, the prodigious muscular power which nature seemed to have bestowed upon his arms, by way of compensation for deficiency in the lower limbs, enabled him to perform many feats of wonderful dexterity where trees or ropes or anything else to climb were in question. At such exercises he certainly much more resembled a squirrel, or a small monkey, than a frog.

I am not able to say with precision from what country Hop-Frog originally came. It was from some barbarous region, however, that no person ever heard of—a vast distance from the court of our king. Hop-Frog, and a young girl by the name of Trippetta, who was a little less dwarfish than he (although of exquisite proportions, and a marvelous dancer), had been snatched away from their families and friends, forcibly carried off from their respective homes in adjoining provinces, and sent as presents to the king by one of his ever-victorious generals.

Under these circumstances, it is no wonder that a close intimacy arose between the two little captives. Indeed, they soon became sworn friends.

Although Hop-Frog was smart and sporty, he was by no means popular, so he did not have it in his power to render Trippetta many services. But she, on account of her grace and exquisite beauty (although a dwarf), was universally admired and petted. As such, she possessed much influence and never failed to use it, whenever she could, for the benefit of Hop-Frog.

On some grand state occasion—I forgot what—the king determined to have a masquerade ball. Whenever a masquerade or anything of that kind occurred at court, the talents of Hop-Frog and Trippetta were sure to be called into play. For this occasion, a gorgeous hall would be fitted up, under Trippetta's eye, with every kind of device that could possibly give striking effect to a masquerade. And Hop-Frog, especially, was so inventive in the way of getting up pageants, suggesting novel characters, and arranging costumes for masked balls, that nothing could be done, it seems, without his assistance.

The whole court was in a fever of expectation. As for costumes and characters, many had made up their minds what roles they should assume a week, or even a month, in advance of the masquerade. In fact, there was not a particle of indecision anywhere—except in the case of the king and his seven ministers.

Why the king and his ministers hesitated I never could tell, unless they did it by way of a joke. More probably, they found it difficult, on account of being so dependent, to make up their minds. In any event, time flew until the night appointed for the party had arrived. As a last resort, the king and his ministers sent for Trippetta and Hop-Frog.

When the two little friends obeyed the summons of the king, they found him sitting and drinking his wine with the seven members of his cabinet council. The monarch appeared to be in a very ill humor. He knew that Hop-Frog was not fond of wine, for it excited the poor cripple almost to madness, and madness is no comfortable feeling. But the king loved his practical jokes, and he took pleasure in forcing Hop-Frog to drink and (as the king called it) 'to be merry'.

"Come here, Hop-Frog," said he, as the jester and his friend entered the room. "Swallow this bumper of wine and then let's have the benefit of your invention."

Hop-Frog showed hesitation.

"We want characters—characters, man—something novel—out of the way. We are wearied with this everlasting sameness. Come—drink! The wine will brighten your wits. Come drink! Drink to your health and to the health of your long-lost friends".

Hop-Frog sighed, but then endeavored, as usual, to get up a jest in reply to these advances from the king, but the effort was too much. It happened to be the poor dwarf's birthday and the command to drink to his 'long-lost friends' forced tears to his eyes. Many large, bitter drops fell into the goblet as he took it, humbly, from the hand of the tyrant.

"Ah! Ha! Ha!" roared the King, as the dwarf reluctantly drained the beaker. "See what a glass of good wine can do! Why, your eyes are shining already!"

Hop-Frog's large eyes gleamed, rather than shone, for the effect of wine on his excitable brain was instantaneous. He placed the goblet nervously on the table and looked round upon the company with a half-insane stare. They all seemed highly amused at the success of the king's 'joke'.

"And now to business," said the prime minister, a very fat and oily man.

"Yes," said the King. "Come, come. Lend us your assistance. Characters, my fine fellow! We stand in need of characters! All of us! Ha-ha! Ha-ha!"

As this was somehow meant for a joke, the king's laugh was chorused by the seven.

Hop-Frog laughed too, although feebly and somewhat vacantly.

"Come, come," said the king, impatiently. "Have you nothing to suggest?"

"I am endeavoring to think of something novel," replied the muddle-minded dwarf, for he was quite bewildered by the wine.

"Endeavoring!" cried the tyrant, fiercely. "What do you mean by that? Ah, I perceive. You are sulky, and want more wine. Here, drink this!" He poured out another goblet full and offered it to the cripple, who merely gazed at it, gasping for breath.

"Drink, I say!" shouted the monster, "or by the devil—"

The dwarf hesitated. The king grew purple with rage. The courtiers smirked. Trippetta, pale as a corpse, advanced to the monarch's seat, and, falling on her knees before him, implored him to spare her friend.

The tyrant regarded her for some moments in evident wonder at her audacity. He seemed quite at a loss what to do or say or how to express his indignation most becomingly. At last, without uttering a syllable, he pushed Trippetta violently from him and threw the contents of the brimming goblet in her face.

The poor girl got up the best she could, and, not daring even to sigh, resumed her position at the foot of the table.

There was dead silence for about half a minute during which time the falling of a leaf, or of a feather, might have been heard. Then the silence was interrupted by a low, but harsh and protracted grating sound, which seemed to come at once from every corner of the room.

"What—what—what are you making that noise for?" demanded the king, turning furiously to the dwarf.

The latter seemed to have recovered, in great measure, from his intoxication, and looking fixedly but quietly into the tyrant's face, merely ejaculated:

"I—I? How could it have been me?"

"The sound appeared to come from without," observed one of the courtiers. "I fancy it was the parrot at the window, whetting his bill upon his cage-wires."

"True," replied the monarch, as if much relieved by the suggestion. "But, on the honor of a knight, I could have sworn that it was the gritting of this vagabond's teeth."

Hereupon the dwarf laughed (the king was too confirmed a joker to object to any one's laughing), and displayed a set of large, powerful, and very repulsive teeth. Moreover, he avowed his perfect willingness to swallow as much wine as desired.

The monarch was pacified, and having drained another bumper with no very perceptible ill effect, Hop-Frog entered at once and with spirit into the plans for the masquerade.

"I cannot tell exactly what spurred the idea," observed he, very tranquilly, and as if he had never tasted wine in his life. "But just after your majesty had struck the girl and thrown the wine in her face—just after your majesty had done this, and while the parrot was making that odd noise outside the window, there came into my mind one of my own country diversions with family and friends. We often enacted this frolic among us at our masquerades, but here it would be altogether new. Unfortunately, however, it requires a company of eight persons and–"

"Here we are!" cried the king, laughing at his acute discovery of the coincidence. "Eight to a fraction—I and my seven ministers. Come! What is the diversion?"

"We call it," replied the cripple, "the Eight Chained Orangutans, and it really is excellent sport if well enacted."

"We will enact it," remarked the king, drawing himself up, and lowering his eyelids.

"The beauty of the game," continued Hop-Frog, "lies in the fright it occasions among the women."

"Capital!" roared in chorus the monarch and his ministry.

"I will equip you as orangutans," proceeded the dwarf. "Leave all that to me. The resemblance shall be so striking that the company of masqueraders will take you for real beasts—and of course, they will be as much terrified as astonished."

"Oh, this is exquisite!" exclaimed the king. "Hop-Frog! I will make a man of you."

"Chains are needed for the purpose of increasing the confusion by their jangling. You are supposed to have escaped, en masse, from your keepers. Your majesty cannot conceive the effect produced at a masquerade by eight chained orangutans, imagined to be real by most of the company, rushing in with savage cries among a crowd of delicately and gorgeously costumed men and women. The contrast is matchless!"

"It must be," said the king, and the council arose hurriedly (as it was growing late) to put in execution the scheme of Hop-Frog.

To costume the king and his courtiers as orangutans, Hop-Frog's mode was very simple, but effective enough for his purposes. Since the animals in question had rarely been seen in any part of the civilized world, the dwarf only needed to make imitations that were sufficiently beast-like and more than sufficiently hideous to secure their truthfulness to nature.

So he first encased the king and his ministers in tight-fitting shirts and drawers, then saturated them with tar. At this stage of the process someone of the party suggested that feathers be used to cover the tar. The dwarf at once overruled the suggestion. He soon convinced the eight that the hair of such a brute as the orangutan was much more efficiently represented by flaxen linen threads. A thick coating of the latter was accordingly plastered upon the coating of tar. As the application of tar and fluff set, Hop-Frog went to get the chain, but first he went to consult with his friend, Trippetta.

The arrangements of the room for the masquerade ball had been left to Trippetta's superintendence, but she was now guided in some last minute particulars by the calmer judgment of her friend, the dwarf.

The grand salon in which the masquerade was about to take place was a circular room with a very lofty, domed ceiling. By day the salon received light of sun through a windowed cupola that extended high above the center of the room, but at night the salon was illuminated principally by a large, candle-laden chandelier that hung by chain from the center of the domed ceiling. The chandelier was lowered or elevated by means of a counter-weight, but so it would not look unsightly, this large weight passed through the ceiling and over the roof.

Hop-Frog insisted, for this occasion, the chandelier be removed. It's waxen drippings (which, in weather so warm, it was quite impossible to prevent) would have been seriously detrimental to the rich dresses of the guests who, on account of the large crowd, could not all be expected to keep away from the center of the salon and out from underneath the chandelier. To make up for the night light the chandelier would have provided, servants set about adding candle sconces at various locations, out of the way, and torches, emitting sweet odor, were placed in the cupped hands of the statues of goddesses circling the salon—some fifty or sixty altogether.

Hop-Frog obtained a long chain and returned to the king and his councilors. First, he passed it about the waist of the king, tied it, then about another of the party, and also tied it, then about all successively, in the same manner.

When this chaining arrangement was complete, and the party stood as far apart from each other as possible, they formed a circle. To tidy up and make all things appear natural, Hop-Frog passed the long remainder of chain across the circle in two diameters, making two lines of chain that crossed the center of the circle at right angles.

The masquerade began at its appointed time, but the eight orangutans, taking Hop-Frog's advice, waited patiently until midnight (when the room was thoroughly filled with masqueraders) before making their appearance. No sooner had the clock ceased striking, however, than they rushed, or rather rolled in all together—for the impediments of their chains caused most of the orangutans to fall, and all to stumble as they entered.

The excitement among the masqueraders was great, which filled the heart of the king with glee. As had been anticipated, there were not a few of the guests who supposed the ferocious-looking creatures to be beasts of some kind in reality, if not precisely orangutans. Many of the women swooned with fright, and a general rush was made for the doors. But the king had ordered them to be locked immediately upon his entrance and, at the dwarf's suggestion, Hop-Frog himself had pocketed the keys.

While the noisy commotion was at its height, with all masqueraders attentive only to their own safety (for in fact there was much real danger from the pressure of the excited crowd), the chain by which the chandelier ordinarily hung might have been seen, had anyone been watching, to descend very gradually until its hooked extremity came within three feet of the floor.

Soon after this, the king and his seven friends, having reeled about the hall in all directions, found themselves at length in its center and, of course, in immediate contact with the chain that hung from above. While they were thus situated, the dwarf, who had followed noiselessly at their heels inciting them to keep up the commotion, took hold of the chain that bound them—right at the intersection of the two portions that crossed the circle diametrically and at right angles. Here, rapidly and accurately, Hop-Frog inserted the hook from which the chandelier usually hung. In an instant, by some unseen agency, the chandelier-chain was drawn so far upward as to take the hook out of reach, and, as an inevitable consequence, to drag the orangutans together in close connection, and face to face.

By this time the party masqueraders had recovered in some measure from their alarm and, beginning to regard the whole matter as a well-contrived pleasantry, they set up a loud shout of laughter at the predicament of the apes.

"Leave them to me!" screamed Hop-Frog, his shrill voice easily heard through all the din. "Leave them to me. I fancy I know them. If I can only get a good look at them, I can soon tell who they are."

Here, scrambling atop and over the heads of the crowd, he managed to get to the wall. Seizing a torch from the hands of one of the statues, he returned by the same path atop the heads of the crowd to the center of the room. He then leapt with the agility of a monkey upon the kings head. From there he clambered a few feet up the chain, holding down the torch to examine the group of orangutans. Still screaming, he said: "I shall soon find out who they are!"

And now, while the whole assembly (the apes included) was convulsed with laughter, the jester suddenly uttered a shrill whistle. At the sound of his whistle the chain rose upward, ascending about thirty feet, dragging with it the dismayed and struggling orangutans, and leaving them suspended in mid-air between the sky-light and the floor.

Hop-Frog, clinging to the chain as it rose, still maintained his relative position with respect to the eight maskers, and still (as if nothing were the matter) continued to thrust his torch down toward them as though endeavoring to discover who they were. So thoroughly astonished was the whole company at this ascent that a dead silence of about a minute's duration ensued. It was broken by a low, harsh, grating sound, just as had attracted the attention of the king and his councilors when the king threw wine in the face of Trippetta.

But, on the present occasion, there could be no question from where the sound issued. It came from the fang-like teeth of the dwarf, who ground them and gnashed them as he foamed at the mouth.

Ruled now, not by the king, but by resentment and seething anger, Hop-Frog glared with maniacal rage into the upturned faces of the king and his seven companions.

"Ah, ha!" said the infuriated jester. "Ah, ha! I begin to see who these people are now!"

Here, pretending to scrutinize the king more closely, he held the blazing torch up close to the flaxen coat that enveloped the king, which provoked the coat to instantly burst into a sheet of vivid flame.

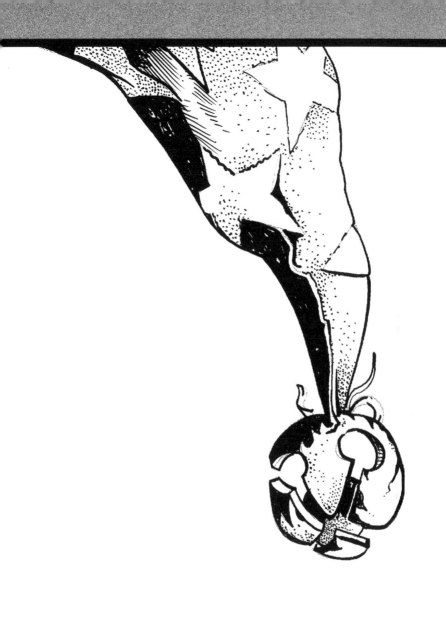

In less than half a minute the whole eight orangutans were blazing fiercely, amid the shrieks of the multitude that gazed at them from below, horror-stricken, and without the power to render them the slightest assistance.

At length, the flames, suddenly increasing in virulence, forced the jester to climb higher up the chain to be out of their reach. As he made this movement, the crowd again sank, for a brief instant, into silence. The dwarf seized this opportunity and once more spoke:

"I now see distinctly," he said, "what manner of people these maskers are. They are a great king and his seven privy-councilors—a king, who does not scruple to strike a defenseless girl, and his seven councilors who abet him in the outrage. As for me, I am simply Hop-Frog, the jester— and this is my last jest."

Owing to the high combustibility of both the flax and the tar to which it adhered, the dwarf had scarcely made an end of his brief speech before the consuming work of the flames was complete. The eight corpses swung in their chains, a stinking, blackened, hideous, and indistinguishable mass. The cripple hurled his torch at them, clambered leisurely to the ceiling, and disappeared through the skylight.

It is supposed that Trippetta, stationed on the roof of the salon, had been the accomplice of her friend in his fiery revenge, and that, together, they effected their escape to their own country—for neither was seen again.

the end

HOP-FROG

Published in 1849, Hop-Frog was probably the last story Poe wrote before he mysteriously collapsed and died in Baltimore at the age of 40. Poe wrote Hop-Frog quickly to pick up a little needed cash from a small, literary magazine. But even though it was a hasty endeavor, Hop-Frog did not disappoint. It is fast-paced and gripping, and many facets of the story, including the issues of injustice, bullying, and revenge are thought-provoking and ripe for discussion

It is said Hop-Frog's resentment and his reaction to ill-treatment imitated Poe's own resentment and fantasized reaction to being underpaid for his literary works. Hop-Frog might also provide a little insight into Poe's battle with alcohol. Poe is often characterized as a problem drinker, but it's likely his actual issue with alcohol was akin to Hop-Frog's; it wasn't that Poe drank so much, it was that his system could handle so little.

Almost everyone can empathize with Hop-Frog's resentment over his captivity and the inhuman treatment that he and his friend Trippetta received from the king and the councilors of the court. At the same time, not everyone would condone how Hop-Frog retaliated against his captors. Poe's stories often stir debate, as this one surely has and does over the appropriateness of revenge.

No doubt, Hop-Frog is a disturbing tale. It is a story about maltreatment and revenge, and true to Poe's typical story-telling mode, the climax of Hop-Frog is particularly disturbing. But also typical for Poe, his Hop-Frog tale is compelling throughout. As always, Poe wrote a story that grabs the reader's attention at the start and holds it to the finish.

THE SYSTEM OF
DR. TARR AND
PROFESSOR FETHER

While on a tour through the southern provinces of France, I came within a few miles of a certain private madhouse, the House of Health. I had heard much about it from my medical friends. Since I had never visited a place of this kind before, my proximity to it on this tour was an opportunity too good to pass up. I proposed to my traveling companion (a gentleman with whom I had made casual acquaintance a few days before) that we should turn aside for an hour or so and look through this establishment. He objected to my proposition; he said he was in a hurry. But he also admitted he would be horrified at the sight of a lunatic.

He begged me, however, to go off on my own to visit the institution; he did not want to interfere with the satisfaction of my curiosity. He counter-proposed that he would ride leisurely on ahead so I might catch up with him during the day, or, at any event, during the next day. I accepted his offer with minimal reluctance.

But just as he was saying good-bye, it occurred to me that there might be some difficulty in obtaining access to the madhouse, so I made haste to mention my fears on this point. He replied that, yes, unless one had either personal knowledge of the superintendent, Monsieur Maillard, or some credential in the way of a letter, there would be difficulty getting in the building to see the place since the regulations of private madhouses were more rigid than public hospital laws. He added, however, that some years ago he had made the acquaintance of Monsieur Maillard, so he would help me gain access to the madhouse by riding up to the door to introduce me. But, he said, the porch would definitely be as far as he would go—no further, no matter what.

Turning from the main road, we entered a grass-grown byway that nearly disappeared as it went forward into a dense forest. We rode some two miles through this dank and gloomy forest before the House of Health came into view. It was a fantastic chateau, poised at the foot of a mountain. But it was much dilapidated and, by the look of it, scarcely habitable through age and neglect. The look of it frightened me, and I half-resolved to turn back. Soon, however, I grew ashamed of my weakness and proceeded.

As we rode up to the gateway, I saw a man peering through the slightly open gate. An instant afterward he came forth, addressed my companion by name, and cordially shook his hand. It was Monsieur Maillard himself. He was a portly, fine-looking gentleman of the old school, with a polished manner and a certain air of gravity, dignity, and authority that was very impressive.

My friend presented me, mentioned my desire to inspect the establishment, and received Monsieur Maillard's assurance that he would show me all attention. My friend then took leave and I never saw him again.

When he had gone, Monsieur Maillard ushered me into a small and exceedingly neat parlor. Among other indications of refined taste, the parlor contained many books, drawings, pots of flowers, and musical instruments. A cheerful fire blazed upon the hearth. A young and very beautiful woman sat at a piano, singing. At my entrance, she paused in her song and received me with graceful courtesy. She was dressed as if in deep mourning. Her voice was low and her manner mild. I thought I detected traces of sorrow in her face, which was excessively, though not unpleasingly, pale. Her appearance excited in me a mingled feeling of respect, interest, and admiration.

In Paris I had heard that Monsieur Maillard managed the institution with the "system of soothing"—that all punishments were avoided—that even confinement was seldom resorted to. The patients, while secretly watched, were left much liberty, and most of them were permitted to roam about the house and grounds in the ordinary apparel of persons in right mind. Having heard this, I was cautious in the company of the young lady, for I could not be sure that she was sane. In fact, there was a certain restless brilliancy about her eyes which half led me to imagine she was not.

Therefore, I confined my remarks to general topics that I thought would not be displeasing or exciting, even to a lunatic. She replied in a perfectly rational manner to all that I said; even her original observations were marked with the soundest good sense.

A long acquaintance with abnormal psychology had taught me to put no faith in mere evidence of sanity, so I continued to practice caution throughout the conversation. Presently a smart footman in tails brought in a tray with fruit, wine, and other refreshments, all of which I accepted and sampled. Soon afterward the lady left the room and, as she departed, I turned inquiring eyes toward my host.

"No," he said. "Oh, no—she is a member of my family—my niece! She is a most accomplished woman."

"I beg a thousand pardons for the suspicion," I replied. "But of course, the excellent administration of your affairs here is well understood in Paris, and I thought it just possible, you know—

"Yes—say no more! I should thank you for the commend-able prudence you have just displayed. We seldom find so much forethought in young men. While my former system was in operation and my patients were permitted the priv-ilege of roaming to and fro at will, too often visitors who requested to inspect the house were careless in what they said and did, and that aroused my patients to a dangerous frenzy. I was obliged to enforce a rigid system of exclusion with respect to visitors, and now nobody whose discretion I cannot rely upon gains access to the premises."

"What do you mean when you say 'while the former system was in operation'? Do I understand you to say that the 'soothing system' of which I have heard so much is no longer in force?"

"We renounced it several weeks ago," he replied.

"Indeed! I am astonished to hear that!"

"We found it, sir," he said, with a sigh, "absolutely necessary to return to the old methods. The soothing system was at all times dangerous, and its advantages have been much overrated. I believe, sir, it was given a fair trial in this house. We did everything that rational humanity could suggest. I am sorry that you could not have paid us a visit at an earlier period so you might have judged for yourself. But I presume you are familiar with the soothing practice— with its details."

"Not altogether. What I heard was at third or fourth hand."

"I shall state then, in general terms, the system is one in which the patients were household-humored; we would not contradict any fancy that entered the brains of the mad. On the contrary, we not only indulged fancies, we encouraged them, and many of our most permanent cures resulted on account of this. For example, we have had men who fancied themselves chickens. Our cure was to treat that fancy as a

fact and refuse such men any food for a week except what a chicken would eat. In this manner a little corn and gravel were made to perform wonders."

"Did the system only pertain to the acceptance and entertainment of your patient's fantasies?"

"By no means. We put much faith in amusements of a simple kind, such as music, dancing, gymnastic exercises, playing cards, certain classes of books, and so forth. We treated each individual as if he or she had nothing more than some ordinary physical disorder, and the word 'lunacy' was never mentioned. And we made a great point that each lunatic should guard the actions of all the others. When you place confidence in the understanding or discretion of a madman, you gain him body and soul. Also, by doing so we were able to dispense with an expensive staff of keepers."

"And you had no punishments of any kind?"

"None."

"And you never confined your patients?"

"Very rarely. Now and then we transported some individual who was heading toward a crisis or already in a fury to a secret cell to make sure his disorder would not infect the rest, and we kept him isolated there until we could dismiss him to family or friends—for we absolutely will not deal with a raging maniac. As it is, a patient like that will usually wind up in a public hospital."

"And you have now changed this system—and you think for the better?"

"Decidedly for the better. The soothing system had its disadvantages, and even its dangers. It has now, happily, been eliminated in all the mental institutions of France."

"I am very much surprised to hear you say that," I said, "for I was sure that method of treatment for mania was the only one used in all parts of the country, including your own institution."

"You are still young, my friend," replied my host, "but the time will come when you will learn to judge for yourself what is going on without trusting the gossip of others. Believe nothing you hear and only half of what you see. As for what we do here at the House of Health, it is clear some ignoramus has misled you. After dinner, however, when you have sufficiently recovered from the fatigue of your ride, I will be happy to take you over to the house and introduce to you a system which, in my opinion—and the opinion of everyone who has witnessed its operation—is incomparably the best ever yet devised."

"Your own system?" I inquired. "A system of your own invention?"

"I am proud," he replied, "to acknowledge that it is—at least in some measure—my own invention. And I will be pleased to demonstrate it to you. But I cannot let you see my patients just now. To a sensitive mind there is always a shock in such exhibitions, and I do not wish to spoil your appetite for dinner. We will dine first—I can give you some veal with cauliflowers in sauce followed by a glass of sherry— and then your nerves will be sufficiently steadied to see them."

I continued to converse with Monsieur Maillard for an hour or two, during which he showed me the gardens and conservatories of the place. At six, dinner was announced, and my host conducted me into a large dining room where many people were assembled. There were twenty-five or thirty people in all, apparently of high rank, certainly of high breeding—although I thought their clothes were too rich, too extravagant. At least two-thirds of these guests were ladies and some were decked-out in clothes that would have been fashionable only many long years ago. Many females, whose age could not have been less than seventy, were bedecked with an overabundance of jewelry, such as rings, bracelets, and earrings, and wore their bosoms and arms shamefully bare. I also observed that very few of the ladies dresses were well made—or, at least, that very few of them fitted the wearers.

In looking about, I discovered the interesting girl to whom Monsieur Maillard had presented me in the little parlor. When I had first seen her she was dressed, most becomingly, in deep mourning attire. But I was greatly surprised to see her wearing an antique hoop skirt with high-heeled shoes and a dirty cap of Brussels lace. The cap was so very much too large for her that it made her face look ridiculously small.

Such was the air of oddity about the dress of the whole party that I began to think the "soothing system" was still in place and that Monsieur Maillard had been willing to deceive me until after dinner so that I would not feel uncomfortable finding myself dining with lunatics. But then I remembered that citizens in the southern provinces of France were known to be peculiarly eccentric and that they held a vast number of old-fashioned notions including, I guessed, their preference for out-dated clothing. Added to that, I found my conversations with several members of the company to be nothing out of the ordinary, so my apprehensions were immediately and fully dispelled.

The room where we dined was sufficiently comfortable and of good dimensions, but there was nothing elegant about it. The floor was bare and the windows were without curtains. The shutters, being shut, were securely fastened with iron bars applied diagonally, after the fashion of shutters on shop windows. The room formed a wing of the grand chateau, so in all, ten windows were on three sides of the room with a door being at the other.

The dining table was superbly set out and loaded with plates that were overloaded with delicacies. The amount of food was absolutely barbaric. Never in all my life had I witnessed so lavish, so wasteful an expenditure of the good things of life. There seemed very little taste, however, in the arrangement of the plates upon the table. In addition, my eyes, which are accustomed to quiet lights, were sadly offended by the oppressive glare of a multitude of wax candles in many silver candelabra that were deposited upon the table and all about the room wherever it was possible to find a place. There were several active servants in attendance, and seated on chairs atop a large table at the far end of the room were seven or eight men with fiddles, fifes, trombones, and a drum. These fellows annoyed me very much during the dinner by an infinite variety of noises which were intended for music, and which appeared to entertain all present—with the exception of myself!

I could not help thinking there was much bizarre about everything I saw—but then the world is made up of all kinds of persons, with all modes of thought and all sorts of customs. As a well-travelled man, I had become quite adept at accommodating a vast assortment of customs, so I took my seat very coolly at the right hand of my host, and, having an excellent appetite, did justice to the good cheer set before me.

The conversation, in the meantime, was spirited and general. The ladies, as usual, talked a great deal. I soon found that nearly all the company was well educated, and my host shared a world of good-humored stories. He seemed quite willing to speak of his position as the superintendent of House of Health, and indeed, the topic of lunacy was, much to my surprise, a favorite one with all present. A great many amusing stories were told having reference to the whims of the patients.

"We had a fellow here once," said a fat little gentleman who sat at my right,—"a fellow that fancied himself a tea-pot. And by the way, don't you think it is especially odd how often this particular notion has entered the brain of the lunatic? There is scarcely an insane asylum in France which cannot supply a human teapot. Our gentleman was a silver teapot, and he was careful to polish himself every morning with buckskin and white chalk."

"And then," said a tall man just opposite us, "we had here, not long ago, a person who had taken it into his head that he was a donkey—which symbolically speaking was quite true. He was a troublesome patient and we had very much to do to keep him within bounds. For a long time he would eat nothing but thistles, but we soon cured him of that idea by insisting upon his eating nothing else. Then he was constantly kicking his heels out like this…"

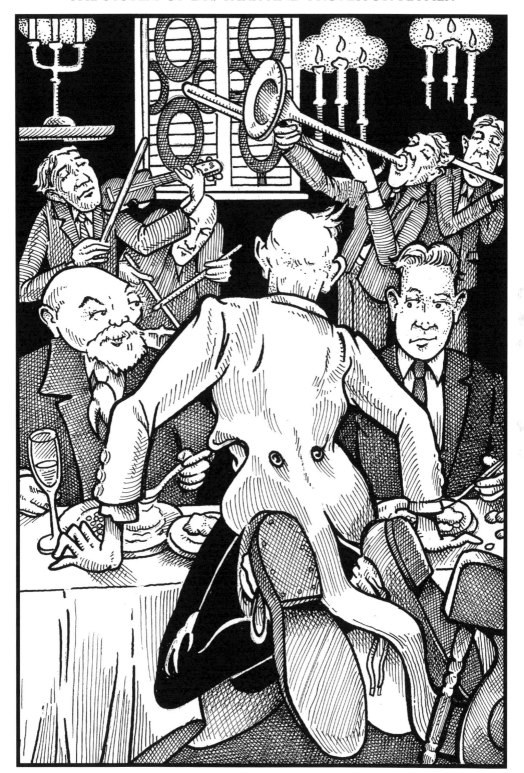

"Mr. De Kock! I will thank you to behave yourself!" interrupted an old lady who sat next to the speaker. "Please keep your feet to yourself! You have put a heel mark on my gown and without doubt a bruise mark on my shin! Is it necessary to illustrate a remark in so practical a style? Our friend here can surely comprehend you without all this demonstration. Upon my word, you are nearly as great a donkey as the poor unfortunate patient imagined himself. Not that your donkey act isn't very natural to you!"

"A thousand pardons, Mademoiselle!" replied Monsieur De Kock. "A thousand pardons! I had no intention of offending Mademoiselle Laplace. Monsieur De Kock will do himself the honor of taking wine with you."

At this Monsieur De Kock bowed down low, kissed his own hand with much ceremony, and took wine with Mademoiselle Laplace.

"Allow me, my friend", said Monsieur Maillard."Allow me to send you a morsel of this veal—you will find it particularly fine."

At this instant three sturdy waiters were succeeding in depositing safely upon the table an enormous dish containing a small calf, roasted whole. It was set upon its knees with an apple in its mouth.

"Thank you, no," I replied. "To say the truth, I am not particularly partial to veal for I do not find it altogether agrees with me. I will change my plate, however, and try some of the rabbit."

There were several side dishes on the table, containing what appeared to be the ordinary French rabbit (this dish is a very delicious treat, which I heartily recommend).

"Pierre," cried the host, "change this gentleman's plate, and give him a side-piece of this rabbit ala cat."

"This what?" said I.

"This rabbit ala cat."

"Why, thank you—upon second thoughts, no. I will just help myself to some of the ham."

There is no knowing, thought I to myself, what one eats at the tables of these country people of the provinces. But I will have none of their rabbit ala cat—and, for the matter of that, none of their cat-ala-rabbit either.

"And then," said a cadaverous looking person near the foot of the table, taking up the thread of the conversation where it had been broken off, "and then, among other oddities, we had a patient, once upon a time, who very stubbornly maintained himself to be a block of cheese and went about with a knife in his hand, soliciting his friends to try a small slice from the middle of his leg."

"He was a great fool, beyond doubt," interposed someone, "but not to be compared with a certain individual whom everybody here but our strange guest knows. I'm talking about the man who took himself for a bottle of champagne and always went off with a pop and a fizz, in this fashion."

Here the speaker, very rudely, I thought, put his right thumb in his left cheek, withdrew it with a sound resembling the popping of a cork, and then, by a movement of the tongue upon the teeth, created a sharp hissing and fizzing imitation of the frothing of champagne. This lasted for several minutes, and I plainly saw it was not very pleasing to Monsieur Maillard. But he said nothing and the conversation was resumed by a very lean little man in a big wig.

"And then there was an ignoramus," said he, "who mistook himself for a frog which, by the way, he resembled in no little degree. I wish you could have seen him, sir,"—here the speaker addressed me—"it would have done your heart good to see the natural airs that he put on. Sir, if that man was not a frog, I can only observe that it is a pity he was not. His croak thus—o-o-o-o-gh–o-o-o-o–gh—was a B-flat, the finest pitch in the world, and when he put his elbows upon the table thus—after taking a glass or two of wine—and distended his mouth, thus, and rolled up his eyes, thus, and winked them with excessive rapidity, thus, why then, sir, I take it upon myself to say, positively, that you would have been lost in admiration at the genius of the man."

"I do not doubt it," I said.

"And then," said somebody else, "then there was Peter Gaillard, who thought he was a booger, and was truly dis-tressed because he could not take himself between his own finger and thumb and roll himself into a ball."

"And then there was Jules Desoul, who was a very singular genius indeed. He went mad with the idea that he was a pumpkin. He endlessly pestered the cook to make him up into pies—a thing which the cook indignantly refused to do. For my part, I am by no means sure that a pumpkin pie—ala Desoul—would not have been very delicious eating indeed!"

"You astonish me with such a distasteful suggestion!" said I, and I looked inquisitively at Monsieur Maillard.

"Ha! ha! ha!" said he. "He! he! he!—Ho! ho! ho!—very good indeed! You must not be astonished, my friend. Our friend here is a wit—a jester—you must not understand him to the letter."

"And then," said some other one of the party,—"then there was Buffoon Le Grand—another extraordinary person in his way. He grew deranged through love and fancied himself possessed of two heads. One of these he maintained to be the head of a philosopher; the other he imagined to be a composite one—a political hack from the top of the forehead to the mouth, and a libel lawyer from the mouth to the chin. It is not impossible that he was wrong, but he would have convinced you of his being in the right, for he was a man of great eloquence. He had an absolute passion for oratory and could not refrain from display. For example, he used to leap upon the dinner-table thus, and–and—"

Here a friend at the side of the speaker, put a hand upon his shoulder and whispered a few words in his ear, upon which he ceased talking with great suddenness and sank back within his chair.

"And then," said the friend who had just whispered to the man, "there was Boullard—the small, spinning top. I call him the 'top' because, in fact, he was seized with the amusing but not altogether irrational notion that he had been converted into one. You would have roared with laughter to see him spin. He would turn round upon one heel by the hour, in this manner—so—"

Here the friend whom he had just interrupted by a whisper performed an exactly similar display himself.

"But then," cried the old lady, at the top of her voice, "your Monsieur Boullard was a madman, and a very silly madman at best; for who, allow me to ask you, ever heard of a human top? The thing is absurd. Madame Joyeuse was a more sensible person, as you know. She had a notion, but it was instinct with common sense and gave pleasure to all who had the honor of her acquaintance. She found, upon mature deliberation, that, by some accident, she had been turned into a rooster, but, as such, she behaved with propriety. She flapped her wings with prodigious effect—so–so— and as for her crow, it was delicious! Cock-a-doodle-doo!– cock-a-doodle-doo!–cock-a-doodle-doodooo-do-o-o-o-o-o-o!"

"Madame Joyeuse, I will thank you to behave yourself!" interrupted our host very angrily. "You can either conduct yourself as a lady should do, or you can quit the table forthwith."

I was much astonished to hear the lady addressed as Madame Joyeuse considering that she had just been describing a Madame Joyeuse herself! She blushed up to the eyebrows, and seemed exceedingly abashed at the reproof. She hung down her head and said not a syllable in reply. But another and younger lady resumed the theme. It was my beautiful girl of the little parlor.

"Oh, Madame Joyeuse was a fool!" she exclaimed, "but there was a lady whose opinions made much sound sense, after all. Eugenie Salsafette was a very beautiful and painfully modest young lady who thought the ordinary mode of clothing herself indecent. She wished to dress, always, by getting outside instead of inside of her clothes. It is a thing very easily done, after all. You have only to do so—and then so—so—so—and then so—so—so—and then—"

"Mon dieu! Mademoiselle Salsafette!" cried a dozen voices at once. "What are you about? Forbear! That is sufficient! We see, very plainly, how dressing yourself outside your clothes is done! Stop! Stop!"

Several persons were already leaping from their seats to withhold Mademoiselle Salsafette from unclothing herself to the end when, without restraint, she stopped herself cold at the sound of a series of loud screams, or yells, from some portion of the main body of the chateau. Likewise, all the other dinner guests stopped all activity at the sound of the screams.

I never saw any set of reasonable people in my life so thoroughly frightened by screams or yells. Yes, my nerves were very much affected by these yells too, but I really pitied the rest of the company. They all grew as pale as so many corpses, and, shrinking within their seats, sat quivering and gibbering with terror, all struck dumb, earnestly listening for a repetition of the sound. It came again—louder and seemingly nearer—and then a third time, very loud. And then a fourth time, but with an evidently diminished vigor. At this apparent dying away of the noise, the company immediately regained its spirit and all was life and stories as before. I now ventured to inquire about the cause of the disturbance.

"A mere trifle," said Monsieur Maillard. "We are used to these things and care really very little about them. The lunatics, every now and then, get up a howl in concert, one starting, then another joining, and so on, as is sometimes the case with a bevy of dogs at night. It occasionally happens, however, that the concert of yells is succeeded by a simultaneous effort at breaking loose. When that happens, of course, it is natural that some little danger would be anticipated."

"And how many patients have you in charge?"

"At present we have not more than ten, altogether."

"Principally females, I presume?"

"Oh, no—every one of them men, and stout fellows too, I can tell you."

"Indeed! I have always understood that the majority of lunatics were of the gentler sex."

"It is generally so, but not always. Some time ago, there were about twenty-seven patients here and, of that number, no less than eighteen were women. But, lately, matters have changed very much, as you see."

"Yes—have changed very much, as you see," interrupted the gentleman who had bruised the shin of Mademoiselle Laplace.

"Yes—have changed very much, as you see!" chimed in the whole company at once.

"Hold your tongues, every one of you!" said my host, in a great rage.

At this the whole company maintained a dead silence for nearly a minute. As for one lady, she obeyed Monsieur Maillard to the letter, and thrusting out her tongue, which was an excessively long one, held it very resignedly with both hands until the end of the entertainment.

"And this gentlewoman," said I, to Monsieur Maillard, bending over and addressing him in a whisper—"this good lady who has just spoken, and who gives us the cock-a-doodle-de-doo—she, I presume, is harmless— quite harmless, eh?"

"Harmless!" exclaimed he, in unfeigned surprise, "why—why, what can you mean?"

"Only slightly touched?" said I, pointing to my head. "I take it for granted that she is not particularly, not dangerously affected, eh?"

"My Gosh! What is it that you imagine? This lady, my particular old friend Madame Joyeuse, is as absolutely sane as I am. She has little eccentricities, to be sure—but then, you know, all old people—all very old people—are more or less eccentric!"

"To be sure," said I, "to be sure—and then the rest of these ladies and gentlemen—"

"They are my friends and keepers," interrupted Monsieur Maillard, drawing himself up arrogantly,—"my very good friends and assistants."

"What! All of them? All the women and all the others?"

"Certainly," he said, "we could not do without the women; they are the best lunatic nurses in the world; they have a way of their own, you know; their bright eyes have a marvelous effect—something like the fascination of the snake, you know."

"To be sure", said I, "to be sure! They behave a little odd, eh? They are a little queer, eh? Don't you think so?"

"Odd!—queer!—why, do you really think so? We are not very prudish, to be sure, here in the South of France. We do pretty much as we please—enjoy life and all that sort of thing, you know? And then, perhaps, this vintage wine is a little heady. A little strong, you understand, eh?"

"To be sure," said I,—"to be sure. By the by, Monsieur, did I understand you to say that the system you have adopted, in place of the celebrated soothing system, was one of very rigorous severity?"

"By no means. Our confinement is necessarily close, but the treatment—the medical treatment, I mean—is rather agreeable to the patients than otherwise."

"And you said the new system is one of your own invention?"

"Well, not altogether. Some portions of it are referable to Professor Tarr, of whom you have necessarily heard, and again, there are modifications in my plan which I am happy to acknowledge as belonging of right to the celebrated Fether, with whom, if I mistake not, you have the honor of an intimate acquaintance."

"I am quite ashamed to confess," I replied, "that I have never even heard the names of either gentleman before."

"Good heavens!" ejaculated my host, drawing back his chair abruptly, and uplifting his hands. "I surely do not hear you aright!"

"I am forced to acknowledge my ignorance," I replied.

"You mean to say that you had never heard either of the learned Doctor Tarr, or of the celebrated Professor Fether?"

"May the truth be held inviolate above all things—I confess I have never heard of either. I feel humbled to the dust not to be acquainted with the works of these, no doubt, extraordinary men. I will seek out their writings forthwith and inspect them with deliberate care. Monsieur Maillard, you have really—I must confess it—you have really—made me ashamed of myself!"

And this was the fact.

"Say no more, my good young friend," he said kindly, pressing my hand,—"join me now in a glass of champagne."

We drank. The company followed our example without stint. They chatted—they jested—they laughed—they enacted a thousand absurdities—the fiddles shrieked—the drum row-de-dowed—the trombones bellowed like so many brazen bulls in a pasture.

The whole scene, growing gradually worse and worse as the wines gained the upper hand, became at length a sort of pandemonium in passing.

In the meantime, Monsieur Maillard and myself, with revelers around and between us, continued our conversation at the top of our voices. A word spoken in an ordinary key stood no more chance of being heard than the voice of a fish from the bottom of Niagara Falls.

"And, sir," said I, screaming in his ear, "you mentioned something before dinner about the danger incurred in the old system of soothing. How is that?"

"Yes," he replied, "there was, occasionally, very great danger indeed. There is no accounting for the whims of madmen. And, in my opinion as well as in that of Dr. Tarr and Professor Fether, it is never safe to permit them to run at large unattended. A lunatic may be 'soothed, as it is called, for a time, but in the end, he is very apt to become unruly. His cunning too is great and legendary. If he has a project in view, he conceals his design with a marvelous wisdom. And the skill with which he counterfeits sanity presents one of the most singular problems to psychologists in their study of mind. When a madman appears thoroughly sane, indeed, it is high time to put him in a straitjacket."

"But the danger, my dear sir, of which you were speaking, in your own experience—during your control of this house—have you had practical reason to think liberty hazardous in the case of a lunatic?"

"Here? In my own experience? Why, I may say, yes. For example, not long ago a singular circumstance occurred in this very house. The 'soothing system,' you know, was then in operation, and the patients were at large. They behaved so remarkably well that anyone of good sense might have known some devilish scheme was brewing. And, sure enough, one fine morning the keepers woke up and found themselves bound hand and foot. They were thrown into cells where they were attended as if they were lunatics by the lunatics themselves. The lunatics had taken over the offices and duties of the keepers! "

"You don't tell me so! I never heard of anything so absurd in my life!"

"It's a fact. It all came to pass by means of a stupid fellow—a lunatic—who for some reason had come to believe that he had invented a better system of government—of lunatic government—than any system ever heard of before. He wished to give his invention a trial, I suppose, and so he persuaded the rest of the patients to join him in a conspiracy for the overthrow of the administrators of the institution."

"And he really succeeded?"

"No doubt of it. The keepers and kept were soon made to exchange places. But not exactly either, for the madmen had been 'free' under the 'soothing system', whereas the keepers were immediately shut up in cells and treated, I am sorry to say, in a very degrading manner."

"But I presume a counter-revolution was soon effected. I mean, this condition of things could not have existed for long. The country people in the neighborhood—visitors coming to see the establishment—would have given the alarm."

"There you are wrong. The head rebel was too cunning for that. He admitted no visitors at all—with the exception one day of a very stupid-looking young gentleman of whom he had no reason to be afraid. He let the man in to see the place just to amuse himself—to have a little fun with him. Then as soon as the head rebel had fooled the stupid visitor sufficiently, he let him out and sent him about his business. In the meantime the visitor's horse had been impounded— it was a delicious breed—so the man had to leave on foot."

"And how long, then, did the madmen reign?"

"Oh, a very long time, indeed—a month certainly—how much longer I can't precisely say. In the meantime, the lunatics had a jolly season of it—of that you can be certain. They dumped their own shabby clothes and put on the family wardrobe and jewels. The cellars of the chateau were well stocked with wine, and these madmen are just the kind of devils that know how to drink it. They lived well, I can tell you."

"And the treatment—what was the particular species of treatment which the leader of the rebels put into operation?"

"As I have already observed, a madman is not necessarily a fool. It is my honest opinion that his treatment of the former keepers was a much better treatment than that which it replaced. It was a very capital system indeed— simple—neat—no trouble at all—in fact it was delicious."

Here my host's observations were cut short by another series of loud yells of the same terrifying character as those which had previously alarmed us. This time, however, the yells seemed to proceed from persons who were rapidly approaching.

"Gracious heavens!" I exclaimed—"the lunatics have most undoubtedly broken loose."

"I very much fear it is so," replied Monsieur Maillard, now becoming excessively pale.

He had scarcely finished the sentence before loud shouts and imprecations were heard beneath the windows. Immediately on the heels of these screams, it became evident that some persons outside the dining hall were trying to gain entrance into the room. Some beating on the door with what appeared to be a sledge-hammer began and the shutters began to shake and be wrenched with great violence.

A scene of the most terrible confusion ensued. Monsieur Maillard, to my excessive astonishment, threw himself under the side-board; I had expected he would make an attempt to resolve the situation.

The members of the orchestra, who for the last fifteen minutes had been seemingly too much intoxicated to do duty, now sprang all at once to their feet and to their instruments. Scrambling upon their table, they broke out with one accord into "Yankee Doodle," which they performed, if not exactly in tune, at least with an energy superhuman during the whole of the uproar.

Meantime, the gentleman who had earlier been restrained from imitating a two-headed orator leaped upon the main dining-table among the bottles and glasses. As soon as he fairly settled himself, he commenced a speech which, no doubt, was a very fine one, if it could only have been heard.

At the same moment, the man with the 'spinning top' predilection set himself to spinning around the apartment with immense energy, and with arms outstretched at right angles with his body so that he had all the blurred appearance of a 'spinning top' in fact, and knocked everybody down that happened to get in his way.

And now, too, hearing an incredible popping and fizzing of champagne, I discovered at length that it proceeded from the person who performed the bottle of that delicate drink during dinner. And then, again, the frog-man croaked away as if the salvation of his soul depended upon every note that he uttered. And, in the midst of all this, the continuous braying of a donkey arose over all.

As for my old friend, Madame Joyeuse, I really could have wept for the poor lady, she appeared so terribly perplexed. All she did, however, was to stand up in a corner by the fireplace and sing out incessantly at the top of her voice,"Cock-a-doodle-de-dooooooh!

And now came the catastrophe of the drama. As no resistance, beyond whooping and yelling and cock-a-doodling, was made to stop the party crashers, the ten windows were very speedily, and almost simultaneously, broken into, immediately followed by the door.

I shall never forget the emotions of wonder and horror I felt when I saw, leaping into the room and rushing down among us, a perfect army of what I took to be chimpanzees, orangutans, or big black baboons of the Cape of Good Hope, all of them fighting, stamping, scratching, and howling.

I received a terrible beating from one of these creatures who boxed me as if he had been trained exceedingly well in the sweet science of fisticuffs.

When I was pounded quite enough, I was able to collect myself, roll under a sofa and lay still. After lying there some fifteen minutes, during which time I was all ears as to what was going on in the room, I came to a satisfactory understanding of what was behind this tragedy.

In giving me the account of the lunatic who had excited his fellows to rebellion, Monsieur Maillard had been relating his own exploits. He had, indeed, been the superintendent of the establishment some two or three years before. But when he grew crazy himself, he was committed as a patient to the institution he had once managed. This fact was unknown to the traveling companion who had introduced me to Monsieur Maillard.

Shortly before my arrival, the keepers of the institution, ten in number, were suddenly overpowered by the patients, led by Monsieur Maillard. First the keepers were tarred up well, then carefully feathered, and then shut up in underground cells. They had been so imprisoned for more than a month, during which period Monsieur Maillard had generously allowed them not only the tar and feathers (which constituted his "system"), but some bread and an abundance of water that was pumped on them daily. At length, one of the keepers was able to escape through a sewer pipe and then, as luck would have it, he gave freedom to all the other keepers just as Monsieur Maillard's banquet was in full swing.

All the while I was gaining this understanding from the chaotic chatter in the room, I was also most eager to leave the premises. I knew that nobody there could vouch for my visitor's privileges, so I snuck on hands and knees through the commotion, over the broken door, and out the doorway to effect my escape from the chauteau. As for my horse— well, once out of the building, I didn't even attempt to find it, supposing that...well, just supposing that...you know. As for the rest of my journey to freedom, I ran down the by-way and along the main road for a much longer time than I believed my lungs, heart, and legs could ever last.

Now I am back in Paris, free from danger, and poised upon a somewhat even keel. I have inquired and I can report that the "soothing system," with important modifications, has been resumed at the chateau. Nevertheless, considering everything, I cannot help agreeing with Monsieur Maillard. His own "treatment" was a very capital one of its kind. As he so justly observed, it was "simple--neat--and gave no trouble at all--not the least."

I have only to add that, although I have searched every library in Europe for the works of Doctor Tarr and Professor Fether, I have, up to the present day, utterly failed in my endeavors at procuring an edition.

the end

THE SYSTEM OF DR. TARR
AND PROFESSOR FETHER

A French doctor, Phillipe Penel, devised a gentle system of housing and treating mentally ill patients about 50 years before Poe wrote this story in 1845. Even so, harsh treatment of mental patients persisted in asylums world-wide. Maybe Poe was trying to draw attention to Penel's gentle methods when he used a similar 'soothing' system in his fictional House of Health. Or perhaps not.

To this day scholars who analyze literature or try to psychoanalyze Poe don't know what hidden rationale motivated him to write this story. Some guess Poe was questioning the yet unproven idea that ordinary citizens could effectively govern themselves in a democracy. Others say he was mocking a legal system where criminals, increasingly aware of benign advancements in asylum care, were pleading insanity to avoid punishment in prison. Still others guess that Poe, who endured periodic depression and suicidal tendencies throughout his life, was taking pleasure in highlighting the thin line separating the sane and insane.

Many scholars agree that any of these motivations, or others, either singly or in any combination, are possible. But esteemed Poe scholar Thomas Ollive Mabbott downplays the need to focus on whatever serious intent lies beneath this story, even while conceding that Poe built all his stories on at least one serious, supporting idea.*The System of Dr. Tarr and Professor Fether* simply strikes Mabbott as one of Poe's best humorous stories, and he is perfectly content with that!

EDGAR ALLAN POE

Edgar Allan Poe was a fascinating, superbly talented writer who lived a troubled, unfortunate life. He was born in Boston on January 19, 1809. His father, an actor, abandoned his family when Poe was one year old, and his mother, an actress, died of tuberculosis when he was two. Brought up by foster parents who never adopted him, Poe did not fit in well at home. A gloomy person, Poe also did not fit in well at school, in the military, or within society at large. But he sure could write well. At the age of eighteen he was a published author and by twenty-two he had decided he would make his living as a writer.

Edgar Allan Poe began his literary career as a poet. He believed beauty of sound was the essential element in good poetry. He relied upon beauty of sound while composing his poetry and his prose and, as a highly skilled literary critic, used sound as a criteria to judge the work of others. Poe also believed all literary works should be short. Applying this standard to himself, he became a master of the short poem and the short story. He is universally credited with inventing the detective story and perfecting tales of horror.

Unfortunately, Poe needed to write constantly to avoid extreme poverty. Though well-known and highly respected, he did not achieve fame until after his ill-fated death at the age of forty. He died soon after being discovered unconscious on a street in Baltimore; he was traveling to Philadelphia to get married.

More than a century and a half after his death, Edgar Allan Poe is still popular with readers the world over. He is the only American writer who could rightfully claim to be a master of three separate literary forms—the short story, the short poem, and literary criticism. Poe is best known for "The Raven", a poem widely considered to be the most famous in all of American literature. Poe was honored in Baltimore, the city where he died, when they named their NFL franchise the "Ravens".

Marc Johnson-Pencook is an illustrator, animator, and muralist. He lives in Minneapolis, Minnesota. His illustrations appear in books, periodicals, gallery shows and private collections, and his murals adorn many walls and ceilings in public places and private spaces in the Twin Cities and beyond. In addition, Marc composes and performs rock music—he currently plays drums for "Ozmo Stone"—a rock band based in Minneapolis. Marc can be contacted at: www.illustratormarc.com

Jerome Tiller lives in Minneapolis, Minnesota. He is co-owner of ArtWrite Productions, a publishing company bent on making education and reading more pleasurable for youth. Adapted Classics, an imprint of ArtWrite Productions, uses fine-art illustrations to introduce classic stories to young readers. Learn more about Jerome, his co-owner son Paul, and their company at: artwriteproductions.com and adaptedclassics.com

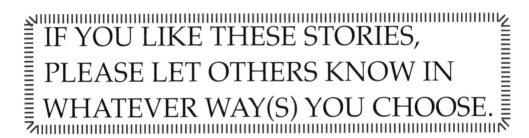